Bouncy Mouse

DATE LOANED	BORROWER'S NAME	DATE RETURNED

DeRubertis, Barbara

Bouncy Mouse

Cover design: Sheryl Kagen

Library of Congress Cataloging-in-Publication Data

DeRubertis, Barbara.
Bouncy Mouse/Barbara deRubertis; illustrated by Eva Vagreti Cockrille.
p.   cm.
"A Let's read together book."

Summary: After being scolded by his father for being too noisy. Boucy Mouse forms
a band that is a big hit at the county fair.
ISBN: 978-1-57565-043-2 (alk. paper)
[1. Bands (Music)-Fiction. 2. Mice-Fiction. 3. Animals-Fiction. 4. Fairs-Fiction 5. Stories- in rhyme.]
I. Vagreti Cockrille, Eva. ill. II. Title.
PZ8.3D455Bo 1998
[E]-dc21   97-44311
                                                            CIP
                                                            AC

10

First published in the United States of America in 1998 by Kane Press, Inc.
Printed in Hong Kong.

www.kanepress.com

Bouncy is a
jumping mouse.
He likes to bounce
around the house.

He likes to sing.
He's very proud
that he can sing
so very loud!

He also thumps
and bumps and drums.
He rat-a-tats and
rum-a-tums.

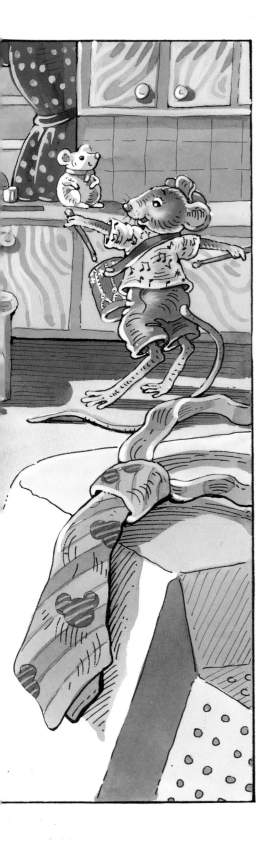

But Dad does NOT
like all the noise.
He says, "Please play
with quiet toys!

"If you must use
your noisy voice,
then go outside.
You make the choice."

So Bouncy says,
"I will go out
where I can bounce
and sing and shout.

"I will go out
where I can drum
and rat-a-tat
and rum-a-tum."

As Bouncy sings and
bounds around,
he hears another
sound . . . a hound!

Howie Hound
has come to play.
He howls and yowls
the hound dog way.

Howie says,
"I like your song."
Bouncy says,
"Then sing along!"

So Howie plays
guitar and howls.
He shakes his hips
and yips and yowls.

Bouncy Mouse
says, "Wow! What fun!
We're sounding GOOD
with one plus one!"

Bouncy then
says, "We can be
the best *duet*
in history!"

Who's coming now?
They moan and groan.
It's Brownie Cow
with her trombone!

Can Brownie play?
She can! And how!
She is a most
astounding cow!

Then Brownie sings
with moody "Moos."
Her trombone slides.
She plays the blues!

Bouncy Mouse
says, "Wow! What fun!
A BETTER sound
is two plus one!"

So Bouncy says
to Brownie Cow,
"Join in! We'll be
a *trio* now!"

Brownie slides
and Howie strums.
Bouncy pats
and pounds the drums.

They're movin' and
they're groovin' now.
And look who's coming!
Rowdy Sow!

Rowdy Sow has
brought her fiddle.
Rowdy jumps right
in the middle.

Rowdy makes a
plunky sound.
She spins that fiddle
right around!

Howie loudly
howls, "We're movin'!"
Brownie proudly
shouts, "We're groovin'!"

Bouncy Mouse
says, "Wow! What fun!
We sound the BEST
with three plus one!"

Bouncy then
says, "We can be
the best *quartet*
in history!"

21

"No doubt about it,"
says a voice.
"And now you have
another choice."

It's Scowly Owl!
The music stops.
He swoops down to
the ground and hops.

Bouncy hides.
What should he do?
He does not want
to be mouse stew!

The owl speaks with
a scowly frown.
"Bouncy, you should
go to town.

"The county fair
begins today.
Those folks would like
to hear you play."

Then Scowly Owl
does something grand.
He smiles! And then
shakes Bouncy's hand!

The quartet marches
into town.
The crowd goes wild!
They boogie down!

Brownie slides,
and Howie strums.
Rowdy plunks,
and Bouncy drums.

Now they're playing
at the fair.
And crowds are shouting
everywhere!

This little mouse
is famous now.
So are the hound
and cow and sow.

But now when Bouncy
Mouse is loud,
his dad says, "Bouncy
makes me proud!"